ENDU___ _

J. Dander

Hear as I say in reality,

Don't do as I write in fantasy.

J.D.

J. Dander
Endure Her
© 2019, J. Dander
Red Ant Publishing
info@RedAntPublishing.com

There are stories nobody wants to talk out about.

This is one of them.

I met Eleanor in 2001.

Though old, she was very much alive. She made me promise to tell her story, the real one, raw and uncut.

I told her some stories were better when left untold, but she didn't agree:

"People always hide behind ethicality and profanity. It's *invalidating*.

It was *my* life, and *I* am no longer ashamed of it.

Life isn't a book of regulations, carefully written without any flaw.

You get into situations you never imagined.

Situations in which you're confronted with that one reality.

The stronger 'win', and the gentler don't *have* the luxury of choice.

In the world I was in, I *chose to fight*, even when it meant, I had *to consent*."

A dark figure, grim and threatening, appeared in the opening of the doorway. The cold flickering lights from the hallway emphasized its shadow and made it more spine-chilling than the image itself. The shade of her long legs stretched into her thin physique, giving it an alien-like appearance.

Eleanor gasped and squeezed her eyes to see who it was. Long legs, a tiny waste, lustrous curls underneath a dainty cap.

It was the stern Aufseherin.

Her captivating look could have made her look like a tender bird, only it didn't. She stepped forward with a sense of entitlement. Her baton hung down along her alluring calves, that were wrapped in silk stockings. The heels of her boots clicked on the tiled floor as she entered the room. With prying eyes and a mean smile, she focused in on Eleanor's frame.

She drew closer, like a bloodhound drawn to injured prey.

Eleanor stood there like a clipped bird, naked and crouched together in a vain attempt to protect her core from the cold.

The Aufseherin stood in front of Eleanor. Her legs were spread, ready to tear up everything in her way. She grabbed Eleanor's hair and pulled it closer to her own. They were standing nose to nose. Eleanor could see her every mark and wrinkle.

As soon as the Aufseherin noticed that Eleanor was studying her, she spit Eleanor in her face.

"You, little Jew whore," spoke the Aufseherin pinching Eleanor's cheek.

Eleanor remained silent.

The Aufseherin yanked Eleanor out of balance and followed up with a punching. She hit Eleanor's breasts and cheeks repetitively with open hand. "Answer me when I ask you a question." Her tone was dark and dangerous.

Eleanor gulped as the burning sensation of the blows cut through her tissue. The Aufseherin laughed and dragged Eleanor by the hair to the table and bend her over with her cheek flat on the bench.

The Aufseherin lifted the baton above her head and smacked it on Eleanor's bare butt.

Eleanor shrieked. She tried to lift her upper body up, but the Aufseherin held her down and continued spanking till Eleanor let out excruciating cries for mercy.

"Where do you think you're going?" snarled the Aufseherin as Eleanor tried to flee from her grip. "Get down immediately or I'll goddamn *make* you!"

Eleanor panicked. She couldn't fight her instincts any longer. She ran towards the door, but no matter how hard she pulled the handle and rammed her shoulder against the door, it wouldn't budge. With massive power she banged her clenched fists against its steady wood. Fear and desperation had taken over as she realized that she was at the Aufseherin's mercy. There was *no way out.*

The door of the closet swayed open and snapped Eleanor out of her panic-drenched rush. She had to stay calm. She had to get a grip on her impulses.

She looked at the closet and noticed it exposed an array of torture equipment.

Without hesitating, the Aufseherin took out a long whip with tiny metal balls at the ending. Before Eleanor realized what was about to happen, she felt vicious cuts in her flesh. No matter how hard her cries, the Aufseherin beat harder and harder with shorter breaks. It was as if her lust was translated into a whip-fucking-rhythm.

"That's what we do with little Jew whores around here," laughed the Aufseherin with a voice drenched in bloodlust.

Eleanor's body lacked the energy to resist anything but begging for mercy. The Aufseherin lead her back to the table and forced her on it.

She spread Eleanor's legs and pulled up her arms, stretching them way too high above her head.

The room was silent but the clicking of handcuffs. The Aufseherin pinched Eleanor, twisted her skin on random spots, and scratched her with her long, red, fingernails.

The Aufseherin picked up a notepad.

 "So, number 46312. Tell me. Have you been a good girl?"

 Eleanor knew better than to ignore her. "Yes Aufseherin," she responded. She tried to hide her pain, for she knew very well, that showing weakness would be yet another invitation to another beating.

"Really?" asked the Aufseherin, while twisting Eleanor's nipple. "I'll ask you again," she continued. "Have you been a good girl, number 46312?"

Eleanor understood very well that *all* answers would lead to punishment. All she could do, was play along and give that sadistic succubus the satisfaction she was looking for.

"No Aufseherin," muttered Eleanor.

"No Aufseherin, *what*?" bossed the Aufseherin hoarse and threatening.

"No Aufseherin. I have been very bad," guessed Eleanor while her muscles tensed, bracing for impact.

The Aufseherin smacked Eleanor ruthless in her face. The sound of impact was as numbing as the blow itself.

"Bad girl! *Bad* girl!" spoke the Aufseherin slow and articulate.

She put a hand on Eleanor's throat, and shifted her weight to her hand to cut off Eleanor's air supply. Eleanor had not seen it coming, nor did her body that was forcefully trying to clear the passage to her lungs. She gurgled and coughed, tensing her constrained muscles.

Her restrained motions were yet another invitation for the Aufseherin to clench her bestial hands even tighter around Eleanor's throat.

"Be good and you might live to see the morning," she hissed stern, with a tone that betrayed her pleasure.

Rather abrupt she let go of Eleanor's neck and entered an endless state of slapping. Eleanor's face, her legs, and already sore breasts were beaten over and over again.

"I'm pretty sure, I asked you a question, *cunt*. Answer me."

She let go of Eleanor's throat and Eleanor tried to speak, but she was still choking and gasping for air. The Aufseherin clenched her fists and pressed it into Eleanor's flesh.

"I will be a good girl. I will be a good girl," begged Eleanor hoping to put an end to the abuse. The Aufseherin however, was far from done.

The Aufseherin tilted the bench, and lowered Eleanor's upper body. Eleanor felt the pressure of the blood rushing down to her head as she laid there with her head hanging down.

"Please stop," she begged, but within seconds, the Aufseherin grabbed Eleanor's hair. "Last warning or I'll make you beg me to *end you*..."

Eleanor nodded, still mastering her cough as the Aufseherin walked to the closet and took a small cane from the shelf. Her stride was decisive, seductive, and slow.

She positioned herself right behind Eleanor's head and lifted her grey calotte skirt. She took off her panties and sat her puss down on Eleanor's face.

"Lick it whore," she commanded.

Eleanor stuck out her tongue, and gently touched the Aufseherin's inner lips. The Aufseherin, annoyed by the delay, wacked Eleanor with her cane.

"Lick me Jew-whore," she ordered, riding Eleanor's face.

Eleanor pulled herself together and licked right between the Aufseherin's pink shields. She took the outer lips in her mouth, and sucked and nibbled, while trying to avoid the under-trimmed bush covering the Aufseherin's slit.

Eleanor managed to ignore her taste, but it was impossible to avoid the smell of half-a-day's sweat, which penetrated her nose and skin.

It all didn't matter. Refusing wasn't an option. Eleanor did what was expected of her. She licked and munched and swirled her tongue to pleasure the Aufseherin in any way she could think of.

The Aufseherin, deeply aroused by the licking, rippled her cunt against Eleanor's face. She turned rounds with her pelvis and grinded her swollen clit against Eleanor's lips. Now and then she would get up to show her superiority by looking down on Eleanor, and after a bout of slapping and choking her, she would return to grinding Eleanor's lips.

The Aufseherin was a sadist without any boundaries. Each time that Eleanor's distress could be increased, she grinned with pleasure.

She enjoyed closing Eleanor's nose and mouth, and deeply savored Eleanor's pleading eyes, begging for a chance to breath.

Eleanor was adapting to the Aufseherin's rhythm. She knew when to gasp for air, when to expect a forceful blow, and when the Aufseherin would launch an attack of snaring and degrading comments.

The Aufseherin's thrusts became deeper and longer and without any shame, she dropped her full weight on Eleanor's face and rode her like a cowgirl. She ragged and ruffled till her juices dripped all over Eleanor's lips.

The Aufseherin rose and looked down at Eleanor, who was tightly tied to the bench and covered in her juices.

Satisfied she lifted her cane and punished Eleanor for all the things she did wrong. For being a Jew-whore. For not responding in the right way. For her defiance and resistance before submission, and, for her submission, which proved she was even a bigger slut than was to be expected.

Eleanor clenched her body in an attempt to phase out the pain that was fired upon her. Blow after blow. Hit after hit.

The Aufseherin looked at Eleanor's meandering body and smiled. With a gratified feminine sway, she walked towards the door and looked over her shoulder.

"You did one thing right, you little cunt. You might be a Jew-whore but at least you're not a Jew. Be good and I *might* let you live...

The Aufseherin left the room. "Take her to the barracks with the other scum," she ordered.

Within seconds two guards entered. They untied her and dragged her to the sleeping-barracks where the other women were hold captive.

They ditched her in a corner, abused, naked and exhausted. They threw some cloths on her and locked the door behind them.

Broken she laid in the corner, ditched, like a worthless bag of garbage, too bruised to raise herself.

A group of women helped her up and cleaned her bruises with the little they had on them. Eleanor, exhausted, drifted off, and fell asleep.

After only a few hours, two thin faces stared at her.

"Come, get up. Hurry."

Eleanor, still dazed, opened her eyes and looked around. Everywhere she looked were women. Packed together, crammed and stacked in bunk beds that did not even give room to a quarter of them. Tangled like a jigsaw, head to feet, like chicken in a cage.

The doors to the barracks opened. Guards entered and spurred the women with bats and barking dogs out of their quarters. Eleanor tried to blend in with the stream of women, subjugated by the terror and viciousness of the guards.

Her eyes wandered around to catch a gaze of the women around her, but nobody dared to meet her eyes.

"I'm Eleanor," whispered Eleanor, offering her hand to another woman after establishing eye contact.

"Frieda." responded the woman fathoming Eleanor, refusing to take her hand.

Eleanor looked at Frieda. There was something different about her. *She* somehow seemed to have a zest for life left in her, hidden somewhere underneath her outer appearance.

"Where are we going?" asked Eleanor.

"Work," responded Frieda.

"Work?" inquired Eleanor.

"Arbeit macht frei, right?" mumbled Frieda.

She looked at Eleanor.

"Sorry. I meant to say slavery," she said, rolling her eyes.

Frieda looked down as they passed several groups of women prodding in different directions.

"Who are they?" asked Eleanor.

"Russians, Jews, more Jews and we, well, *we* are the political prisoners of course. And them," said Frieda, pointing her nose at an enormous group of people, "*Them*, we'll *never* see again."

"What?" pressed Eleanor, since Frieda already regretted prattling and avoided answering altogether.

"Special program they *say...*, *be quiet*," hissed Frieda annoyed, cutting off her own sentence.

"Look down at your feet and *don't* make eye contact," urged Frieda as four Aufseherinnen passed them by, "they kill for less."

Loud screams prevented Frieda from elaborating. One of the female guards pulled a woman out of the group of Russians and dragged her to the ground. As soon as the woman was down, the Aufseherinnen battered and kicked her for no reason other than that they could.

It was a young woman, close to twenty. Her head was shaven to take away her feminine appearance.

Her cries resonated in the streets as the guards kicked her in her face and tortured her with sticks. They called her names and enjoyed *their* power and *her* misery.

"*Wait, wait…*," roared one of the female guards with laughter, "*Look!*"

The guard jumped up in the air, and landed as hard as she could on the knee of the poor woman. The woman exclaimed bone-chilling howls as her knee got scattered into pieces.

Eleanor stepped forward but Frieda pulled her back. "There are other ways. For her it's already too late…"

Eleanor stomach turned as her inner cries found a way out through her tear ducts. It was wrong and unjust. What miserable creatures treat people like this? How could anyone feel such disdain and hatred towards anyone that torture became fun? Where on earth did this malice come from?

"Any volunteers?" joked one of the female guards, claiming their victory. She grabbed a bat to add the final punchline to her joke.

With ferocious blows she hit the woman on her head. Her blood, brain, and teeth lay scattered all over the street.

Only the noisy giggles coming from the guards, rose above the motionlessness of the ice-cold scenery.

The imprisoned women passed the scene in silence.

They disappeared into the factories where they would slave till deep in the night.

Frieda joined Eleanor as they put on their overalls. She grabbed Eleanor's arm and looked at the red and blue bruises on Eleanor's body.

"What happened?" asked Frieda. "The short version please," she added reading Eleanor's personality.

"My husband has been arrested. A Nazi tried to blackmail me and now I'm trying to survive the *bitches* we're all trying to survive. I guess," she said like she was ordering a loaf of bread.

Frieda observed her as another woman pushed herself between them and faced Frieda. "She is *new. Keep the circle closed,* remember?"

The woman eyeballed Eleanor. Eleanor looked puzzled at Frieda, who in turn nodded at the woman.

Frieda turned her head back to Eleanor. "She thinks you're a *spy. Are you?*"

Eleanor laughed at Frieda. "No, I am not, but wouldn't anybody say that?"

"Of course, they would," replied Frieda as if her question still made sense.

The women were forced to their workbenches, where they had to assemble technical equipment into weaponry and armor.

"Would be a shame if someone made a mistake constructing these babies, don't you think?" whispered Frieda, pointing at an explosive. She poked Eleanor in the side.

"Would it?" uttered Eleanor, before realizing what Frieda was actually saying.

"*Damn, too bad*," winked Frieda, *failing* to put together the designator. 'A girl has got to do what a girl has got to do!"

Eleanor's dull expression changed into a spirited one. She knew exactly what to do.

The women worked till deep in the night.

Relieved that they actually made it through another day, they returned to the barracks. Against better judgement, they hoped that today would be the day that they would get something to eat, since for most of them, it had been ages since their last meal, and by their faces, you could tell.

Completely worn out, the women crawled into their bunk-beds to get some rest. In a few hours, another long day would be ahead of them.

Eleanor shared a bed with Frieda and two other women.

After only thirty minutes the door slammed open. A guard entered proclaiming number 46312.

"Number 46312," it echoed through the sheds.

Eleanor gasped and looked at Frieda. It was Eleanor's number. She had to come forward.

"Last chance for number 46312. Show yourself, or we'll –"

A loud crack blared through the air. The girl sleeping in the bed closest to the guard was shot through the head.

"I believe someone was hungry. Be my guest," gimmicked one of the guards pointing at the dead girl.

"Number 46312. I'm not going to ask again," he said.

Eleanor stumbled forward, shaking, as she presented herself.

They grabbed her and dragged her along over the empty streets.

Goose pimples spread over her arms as she realized where they were taking her. She so much hoped *never* to have to go there again, but here she was, caught in that dreadful regimen that started with hosing her down with ice cold water.

She knew she had to take another round of abuse. She *would* have to endure it.

Wet and with palpitating heart she was tied to the bench.

"So, honey. I hear you're good at munching mush," jeered one of the female guards. "Don't think that we don't know that eating pussy makes you all wet and slippery."

She took Eleanor's stiff nipples between her fingers, and was about to squeeze it, as the other guard interrupted her. "Come on, hurry, Lotte will be here soon. *You* can play with her later."

They walked out and closed the door behind them.

After a few minutes the door slammed open and a man and women entered the room.

"This is her," spoke the woman mysterious and giggly.

Eleanor recognized the voice of the Aufseherin.

"That little Jew whore ate out my pussy honey. Aren't you jealous baby?"

The man chuckled as he put his arm around the Aufseherin and kissed her on the lips.

"I love it when you talk to me like that," said the man with a typical German sound.

"Gustav, beast, du bist ein Tier!" giggled the Aufseherin.

Eleanor held her breath. The bitch had a name.

The pair, busy fondling each other, entered the room and moved to the bench Eleanor had been tied to.

They embraced each other as if they were a couple.

The man studied Eleanor.

"She isn't *that* pretty," observed Gustav.

"I didn't say she was, did I?" chuckled Lotte.

"No, but you didn't call her an ugly dog either," he grinned while kissing Lotte on the cheek. "Look at all that fat over here," he chortled while pulling Eleanor's skin. "Time for das Ravensbrück diet, don't you think?"

Both of them chortled.

"Gustav, you have to admit there is something cute about her. Look at that submissive little cunt," blurted Lotte out while smacking Gustav's ass.

Gustav looked deep in Lotte's eyes and put his hand in her panties. He rubbed and stroked Lotte's pussy until her cunt was all mushy and wet. He took out his fingers, dripping from Lotte's juices and propelled them in Eleanor's mouth.

"Suck it you little hussy," ordered Gustav while rubbing his hand over her lips and chin.

"Tell her Gustav, tell her what a hussy she is," glowed Lotte while grinding her horny body against him.

Eleanor couldn't believe it. Weren't there any rules about this in the Geneva convention?

Lotte climbed on Eleanor's bare body and sat on her pelvis, "Come on Gustav, don't you want to aboard number 46312?" whispered Lotte coy while rubbing Eleanor's tits.

"Of course, I do sugar-tits. Show me what to do with her," encouraged Gustav.

Lotte leaned backwards and twisted Eleanor's nipple till the skin of her breasts was about to be torn off.

Eleanor gave a shrilling cry.

"So, you wanna know what to do with her?" giggled Lotte with a pleasurable voice. "I'll show you."

She rubbed Eleanor's skin like she was actually trying to pleasure her and turned around on Eleanor's pelvis. She grinded Eleanor's pussy with her pelvis and slapped it before hopping off to the closet. She grabbed a cane and a wooden bat.

She walked back to the bench, slapping the cane seductively in her hand.

As if it was a natural thing to do, she hopped back on Eleanor's pelvis and lifted the cane above her head.

She dropped the cane on Eleanor's legs. Eleanor cringed and her face jolted as the impact left a stinging red mark.

Lotte loved the change of color and turned it into a project. She created an artistic pattern of naturel and flashing skin, while making fun of Eleanor's grunts and screams. One smack after the other. On her arms, her legs, her breast, her belly, not even her feet were safe from the sharp blasts of impact.

"Are you wet yet, you little cock whore?" laughed Lotte, scratching Eleanor's belly while kissing Gustav.

Lotte and Gustav grabbed Eleanor by her shoulders and pulled her higher up the bench till her head was tilted back down the top of the bench, exposing her neck.

Lotte turned her back towards Eleanor's face, and bend over at the head of the bench. She stepped backwards and pressed her pussy in Eleanor's face. "Lick it bitch, lick it," she bossed while pushing her pussy firmly against Eleanor's face.

"Look how much that little hussy loves sucking my wet cunt, baby," Lotte rejoiced while rubbing her clit against Eleanor's lips.

"Hit her Gustav. Spank that tramp," hurried Lotte aroused, handing him the cane.

Gustav's eyes twinkled upon hearing Lotte's encouragements. It spurred him to continue spanking and caning until Eleanor's grunts and shivers had made Lotte come. Her juices squirted out of her muff. Her facial expression cramped as if it was carved out of stone.

She sighed satisfied, as the warm stirring tension left her body, and a tranquil silence mastered her.

She looked at Gustav with a look that showed she was up to something. Lotte had come, but was *far* from done.

"Let's switch places Hitler-boy," laughed Lotte euphoric. "I want to see how well you can fuck that little slut in her mouth. *Fuck her whore-throat Gustav*," she roused.

Gustav dropped his cane to the ground and looked at Lotte. "She wants it, doesn't she?" Gustave grinned turning to Eleanor. "You want it don't you? *Don't you, you stupid cunt*?"

Eleanor was too apathetic to respond because Gustav, without any leniency, hit her in the face yelling, "Answer me slut! *Answer me!*"

"Yes, yes," whispered Eleanor dull. "Yes, I want it."

Using words that weren't hers, were natural to her. First Paul, now Gustav and Lotte. It was what she had to do to stay alive.

Gustav pulled Eleanor's head further backwards so he could access her throat with his dick. He enjoyed the sight of the helpless women in front of him, and he couldn't help but savoring the view before pressing his cock in her mouth. He pushed and jostled it in till he touched the back of her throat with the tip of his cock.

He looked at her as he held his cock in place. They heard the saliva gurgling in her mouth as he fucked her throat, pushing his cock further beyond his natural length.

He savored the warmth and smoothness of her throat while pressing her lips and face against his crotch to show his domination. Lotte loved what she saw and could not resist opening Eleanor's legs further so she could pat Eleanor's pink and swollen pussy lips. Eleanor's pussy gulped with glittering wetness.

Lotte pressed the thinner side of the cold bat against Eleanor's legs and pressed its top against her slippery slit.

She hesitated for a brief moment, but everyone in the room knew what was about to happen as she looked at the bat and the inviting pink flesh in front of her.

She kissed Eleanor's clit before pressing the bat into Eleanor's pussy. Deep, till it wouldn't go any deeper. Lotte pulled the bat back and started grappling. She was moving the bat back and forth, in and out of Eleanor's cunt.

It was like Lotte entered an out of body state where Eleanor was no longer her prisoner but a lover to satisfy. "Come on you little bitch," yelled Lotte, "You know you want to come…"

"And, we won't stop till you do," added Gustave, pleasured. "*Come*, or we will continue pounding you till both your cunt and throat are raw and bloody."

"Oh Gustav, *you sexy beast*, tell her," said Lotte as she rubbed her own clit with her fingers.

Eleanor felt the pain increasing as Lotte kept thrusting the bat in and out of her pussy.

It was like a rock-hard cock pounding her insane. Eleanor lost all focus as they were drilling her on both sides. On one side Gustav, who was fucking her throat and cutting off her air supply with his hand and dick. On the other side Lotte, fucking her pussy with the bat.

Eleanor felt how her pussy turned raw, and how her fluids were no longer able to support the friction. Her body was worn out by the two-sided thrusting, spanking and choking, and she knew this was only the beginning if she didn't climax. She would *have to* come.

She tensed her pelvic muscles and focused on her memories of William. William, *her* William. She remembered how the weight of his body felt on top of her. How his hands touched her body, and how the warm tones of his voice touched her ear. It was his voice, his warm and caring voice that resonated in her ears.

Gustav's poking burned and numbed her throat.

Eleanor gurgled. She was unable to spit as she hung there upside down, unable to move her head.

She remembered her husband's warmth, his breath, his loving touch, and as if it was reality, she felt his soft lips on hers.

 As she drifted off, and her lips tried to shout out his name, she reached a sexual peak. Gustav closed her nose and throat and the lack of oxygen opened a new world of never-ending space and ecstasy.

Gustav felt how her throat opened, intensifying his experience, and in response he blew his seed as deep in her throat as he could.

Little drops of Eleanor's spit, mixed with blood and cum, dripped out of her mouth down her nose and face.

Lotte was still fucking her. Not for pleasure but to torment. Eleanor's body, weary from the deep hard impacts of the inflexible cock-like object, shaped her cunt to its form, instead of a cock that bends to the walls of her moist cave.

"Mount her again Gustav, *please*," moaned Lotte as she withdrew the bat from Eleanor's pussy.

As Lotte licked the tip of the bat, Gustav grinned. He grabbed Lotte and bend her over with her face flat on Eleanor. "*No.* It's *your* turn now, unsatisfiable cock-whore," he whispered as he put his half-hard cock in Lotte's wet snatch.

He held Lotte close as she fucked his cock hard, with deep and intense strokes.

Their entangled bodies bumped over and over against Eleanor until they were again flooded with the warmth and pleasure accompanying sexual satisfaction.

Everybody was sweaty, but it was only Eleanor that was left with goose pimples as Lotte and Gustav straightened their clothes. Gustav, beyond satisfied, looked at Lotte.

"Now what, sugar-tits? Return her to the barracks?"

"But Nein," replied Lotte grinning. "I'm free in the morning. I'll be taking number 46312 for another spin!"

Gustav chuckled. "Who of the two of you, was the slut again?"

Lotte giggled and with twinkling eyes she threw a blanket over Eleanor. "Don't you worry, we're not necrophiliacs, *yet*. And besides, it would be *rude* to let you wait all naked and in the cold..."

The cheerful couple reached for each other and held hands. Relief eased Eleanor's tensed body as they walked out and slammed the door behind them,

Sticky and filthy she laid there. Too stressed and sad to sleep on the hard, cold, bench. Unsure if she should wish for the *night* to be over, she wished for all of it to be over.

Eleanor startled out of a deep sleep as the door swayed open.

"Who the *fuck,* do you think you are?" spoke Lotte while roughly grabbing Eleanor in the middle of her face. "Who the *fuck,* do you think you are?" she repeated, thumping Eleanor's head against the bench.

Eleanor quivered. She had no clue what Lotte was talking about. It had to be yet another trick question.

"I don't know, Aufseherin," responded Eleanor.

"You filthy Jew-whore," continued Lotte. "Did you betray your Aryan husband with a filthy no-good Jew?" she snickered while clenching her thumb and second finger hard in Eleanor's cheek.

"No, I didn't," countered Eleanor still too sleepy to realize what Lotte was talking about.

"Stop lying to me!" shouted Lotte, slapping Eleanor in the face. "Your husband, the SS officer P. Jordan, is looking for his slut-wife, and guess who I have in front of me?"

Eleanor gasped. "*Paul*?"

"Are you denying that you betrayed him? Are you denying to have spread your hungry little legs for that nasty Jew? Can't do that anymore can you, now he's waning away in Auschwitz?" added Lotte venomous.

Eleanor's heart skipped a beat. She missed everything Lotte was saying after *William was in Auschwitz...* In *Auschwitz*, one of the most horrifying places imaginable...

"Boohoo, lost your tongue?" mocked Lotte with a crack in her voice and a smug look on her face. "If *I* had been your husband, and you would have cheated on *me*, I would have let you *rot away* in here.

Then again, maybe not. If you're as good in giving head as eating pussy, I fucking understand your husband and I would be knocking on the god damn gate too."

Eleanor didn't say a thing... Was this her ticket out of here? Was she going to pretend to be Paul's wife?

She detested her thoughts, but she knew this could be her only chance of getting closer to William.

Lotte bend over and stood face to face with Eleanor. "I'm going to miss your slutty little tongue," she whispered. "If you insist I'll let you have a goodbye kiss," chuckled Lotte, lifting up her skirt and lowering herself on Eleanor. "Come on number 46312, you know what I want from you... You don't want a tragic accident to happen to you right before your husband picks you up, don't you?"

Eleanor on automatic pilot, swirled her tongue through Lotte's dense puss. She *could* endure this. She could. Everything would be better soon.

With her puffy mouth and sweet tongue, she circled around Lotte's clit with alternating rhythms and intensities. Lotte's moaning increased as Eleanor build up the tension. Lotte's trembling betrayed her withholding strength about to be released.

Lotte moaned and screamed out of pure pleasure as her muscles tensed and surrendered to her own mechanism, until her fluids gushed over Eleanor's face.

Lotte grinned at Eleanor with a sense of melancholic longing. "You'd better take care, next time I won't let you get away this easily."

The Aufseherin ordered the guards in the hallway to release Eleanor, give her a warm shower and a decent meal.

"Dress her properly, she is one of us now. Her husband will pick her up in the SS residence."

They guided her through long halls to a room where they set up a hot bubbly bath for her. She hesitated in front of the tub. She longed for it, yet it felt like ultimate betrayal. Not only to William, but to all the women in there who were abused, exploited and battered.

Increasing unrest in her stomach spread to the rest of her limbs as she stood there. *Paul*, what was she going to do with *Paul*?

The door opened and a pretty girl with long dark braided hair stepped in. She looked at Eleanor. As their gaze met, she immediately casted her eyes at Eleanor's feet. "Please miss, if you get into the tub, I will wash you."

Eleanor looked at the little girl, who helped her out of her cloths and into the tub.

The little girl, paying attention to every detail, noticed the water was too hot.

Afraid for punishment, she immediately added cold water.

Eleanor's body woke up from its freezing rest. She smiled at the girl and closed her eyes as the subtle warmth of the bath embraced her. The girl washed Eleanor's face and shoulders with a wet cloth.

It relaxed her, though her inner restlessness challenged the temporary ease of her new status quo. The firm grip of anxiety held on to her as she tried to free herself from the overwhelming thoughts of what laid ahead.

She promised herself one thing. She would take advantage of *everything* they offered. She would take it all, and then *fight*. *Fight* for her life, *fight* for her husband, *fight* for her country and all she held dear.

After the warm bath, the girl laid out fashionable clothes and set up a copious dinner. Eleanor ate more than she could, and stuffed her pockets with the remaining food.

The little girl re-entered and blushed, trying to hide her smile.

Eleanor realized she looked rather foolish in her formfitting coat, with bulges of food in each of her pockets. She smiled back at the girl and observed her.

"Hungry?"

The little girl nodded.

Eleanor took the food from her pockets and told the girl to eat.

"I am not allowed to," stammered the girl.

"I won't tell," whispered Eleanor. "Quick, have some."

It was *all* the girl needed to stuff her face with everything she could get her hands on. The girl, with cheeks loaded like a chipmunk, startled as they heard a loud knock on the door.

Eleanor beckoned the girl to hide under the table.

"Come in," replied Eleanor like she belonged there.

A male guard entered. "I'm here to take you to the officer's residence, mam."

"I'll be out shortly," replied Eleanor as she sent him out of her room.

Eleanor kneeled and popped her head under the tablecloth. "Almost done?"

She wiped some crumbs off the girl's face. "Oh, and thank you for the warm bath, it was just what I needed."

The girl's dark brown eyes came to life upon Eleanor's loving touch and compliment. "Hang in there little one. It will soon be over."

The girl nodded at Eleanor and rushed out of the room.

Eleanor put on her coat and recalled what she had said. She felt guilty for lying. *It wouldn't all be over soon.*

With dread, she walked towards the door where the guard was waiting for her. As if to delay, her eyes wondered through the room.

Thea butter-knife. She slipped it in one of her pockets. Better be safe than sorry, she thought.

The guard knocked on the door and guided Eleanor through the deserted streets. She could see the burning lights of the factory where the women were still slaving. She withdrew to her thoughts.

"Hey, watch your step," uttered the guard while pushing Eleanor aside. Eleanor looked down and was about to vomit as she was standing next to human remains.

"Take it easy," laughed the guard. "It was just a Jew."

"*Just* a Jew?" snapped Eleanor obstinate. She turned towards him in anger, failing miserably at hiding her true feelings.

The guard looked at her with a held back aggression and disbelief. "*They are not people like me and you. They are animals.* They are tearing our superior society down and weakening our strong bloodline. *You are not a Jew-lover are you?"*

Eleanor rasped, suppressing her true feelings, "Me a Jew lover? Oh, no," she laughed. "Everyone knows that Jews are the rats of this society. Heil Hitler!" Eleanor chuckled uncomfortable, as she closed her feet and raised her right hand.

The guard turned at her, raised his arm and spoke with strong conviction. "Heil Hilter!"

While he kept ranting about the perfect Aryan world they were fighting for, she realized she had to find out more about the camp. It would tell her so much about William's situation.

She touched the guard's arm, and while making light conversation, she asked him for a tour of the compound.

"My husband Officer Jordan would be so pleased if you show me everything there is to know," she added like a perfect little lady.

The guard, looking forward to a prosperous career, became aware of the benefits of her question. He was determined to get ahead, and so began her tour.

Strolling over the depressing roads of the compound, Eleanor wished she never asked.

He showed her everything. From the weaponries and textile factories, to the ovens and chambers where they burned and gassed their prisoners. Eleanor couldn't believe her eyes and ears.

The guard told her without any restrain, pain or remorse, how babies, even new-born, were burned and drowned.

He made fun of 'the bunnies', a group of Polish women, forced to take part in medical experiments, set up by *physicians* and medical companies. The experiments either mutilated or killed the women. And, in case they survived, they were executed like lab-rats.

Everyone in her home city was talking about the horrific things that were taking place in the Nazi camps, but this was beyond imagination.

Lined-up prisoners, forced to stand before graves they had to dig themselves, were shot by the prisoners behind them. They now, were forced to step forwards, and standing in front of their own grave, seconds away from their predecessor's fate...

No longer, was Eleanor able to keep up appearances. She felt sick to her stomach while the guard next to her was still effortless rattling away.

Hasted footsteps and voices, muttering around the corner, drew the attention of the soldier. He ran towards the noise, ready for action, with his gun in front of him, he crossed the street.

Eleanor, nervous and on edge, followed. The soldier's eyes scanned the area until he noticed a tall ladder against one of the camp walls.

Seconds later they were standing eye to eye with a group of people.

Unsure of what to make of it, he held them at gunpoint,

"Hands up or I'll shoot," he threatened.

Caged, the group scanned the area for another way out.

"Raise your hands and drop your weapons or I'll shoot all of you," repeated the guard, preparing to pull the trigger.

Eleanor, hiding behind the capo's back, looked at the poor individuals. They were in serious trouble. Eleanor looked closer and...

"*Frieda?*" Whispered Eleanor.

"I will not repeat myself again," yelled the capo on the breach of an outburst. "Step away from the wall or I'll *end* you right here, right now!"

The group of people stepped away from the ladder.

Reluctant, they put their hands up in the air.

Frieda looked at Eleanor, who dressed up in Nazi-cloths, and decided right there and then that the bitch *was* a traitor after all.

"Look at those stupid rats," laughed the soldier poking Eleanor with his elbow. "I know what is about to happen to them. Unless... Do you want to have a say in it too? Eleanor, must we burn them, drown them, or should we go all lady-like on you and hang them?"

The soldier reached for his pocket and grabbed his whistle to blow the alarm.

He inhaled and was ready to blow, when he felt a cool stump blade cutting through the flesh of his neck. Gushing blood, escaping under pressure, splashed around, and the air in his lungs fizzed up into a gushing stream of red bubbles.

Eleanor stood there trembling and gagging.

In her hands, shaking and trembling, a blood covered knife. She stared at the soldier and at her coat that was completely drenched in his blood.

Though the escapees let out a sigh, Eleanor froze as if she had seen a ghost. Frieda ran towards her and grabbed her by the arm.

"Eleanor are you coming with us?" pressed Frieda.

"Based on your actions you're joining us, based on the way you are dressed, I would guess this is where you belong. Are you an Aufseherin?"

"No, no, *no*, I'm not. Paul thinks I'm his wife but I'm not. They were taking me to him, and—"

"Do you want to? You *will* have some explaining to do with those drenched clothes," said Frieda making haste.

"No, no, absolutely not! He –"

Eleanor was about to elaborate but Frieda grabbed her by the arm and pulled her to the ladder.

Eleanor climbed the ladder like a stiff one-legged pirate, with Frieda closely behind her, pushing her butt with each step.

"*Run Eleanor, run. Follow the others*," yelled Frieda as soon as Eleanor crossed the wall.

Eleanor was running. Running as hard as her feet could carry her. She ran like the wind, though by far not so dainty and athletic as Frieda.

Frieda could have passed Eleanor, but she stayed with her to guide her through.

She respected Eleanor. She never expected a woman like *her* to have the guts to fight for what she believed in.

The forest was getting denser and harder to get through as Frieda looked at Eleanor who was gasping for air.

"Rest a bit, *breathe*. We're at a safe distance now," said Frieda, by no means short of oxygen.

Eleanor stopped and bend over. Her head was spinning as she dropped to the ground.

"Come. Sit, and put your head between your legs. You'll feel better soon."

Frieda was right, after a while, she did feel better.

Eleanor was about to lean back, but Frieda spurred her back on her feet. "I'm sorry Eleanor but we've got to go the camp. Make use of your adrenalin rush now it's still there."

"Camp?" stalled Eleanor.

"Yes, camp, we're going to the Partisans."

"Partisans?" repeated Eleanor, this time truly surprised and not just stalling.

She heard tales about brave partisans fighting Nazis, but she always thought it were wishful Robin Hood stories.

"Yes, we are real," said Frieda looking at Eleanor's reaction. "You're looking at one."

Eleanor's eyes popped out of her face.

Frieda grinned, "That exact look, made me trust you. Nobody is able to fake the-eyes-wide-open   I-cannot-believe-you-just-said-that-look."

Frieda's toughness and sparkling eyes made sense to Eleanor now. This was a woman on a mission. This was a warrior.

They picked up speed and Frieda continued her introduction. "There are quite some groups fighting for freedom. Families, communities, loners, prisoners who managed to escape from the camps or transport…"

"So, everybody works together?" asked Eleanor.

"*No,* it's not like the-enemy-of-my-enemy-is-my-friend," she grinned sceptic. "We all want to defeat the Nazis, but there is a lot of hatred among groups as well."

"*Hatred? Why*?" asked Eleanor.

"People are so easily manipulated. They wake up one morning and fail to see the human behind the projection they themselves forced on them."

Eleanor tried to understand.

It was true what Frieda said. Why did the Nazis shave off their prisoner's hair? To make them less human. Why blame someone else for your misfortune? So, you *yourself* can be part of a group that feels superior to others. Why abuse and manhandle people that could be your parents, your friends or even your little sister?

Fluttering sounds of trucks and motorcycles approached them. Eleanor once again, turned as white as a ghost.

"Don't worry, good people," laughed Frieda comforting. "Behold Elanor, the Partisans."

After a brief introduction, they entered the trucks. Eleanor leaned back. The swirling wind seemed to purposely lift her hair as if to blow away her sorrow. For the first time in a very long time, she experienced a sense of freedom.

They arrived at the camp. The atmosphere was buzzing. It was a strange mix of oppression and cheer. A zillion people were occupied with whatever they thought would help their cause. Hunters, cooks, armories, fighters at a level of professionalism that surprised her. *Most* were professional, she grinned. Definitely not *all*, based on the look of a man, sitting on a crate, just being "*happy*".

Many partisans approached her, and patted her on the back, to thank or welcome her. She observed how they welcomed Frieda, warm and relieved to finally have her back. Frieda was home.

The evening fell and they gathered together around a fire. It was large enough to warm them, yet small enough to prevent detection.

One of the leaders, robust and courageous, stepped forward,

"Let us toast to ending this *bloody* war. Let us honor our friends that are no longer among us, and to you, brave Frieda. To you and your team, who risked their lives *once again* to infiltrate Ravensbrück. Cheers to all the prisoners that you taught to tamper with the designators, and to the many Nazi casualties this will result in. And, let us not forget to welcome our new member Eleanor.

Eleanor, thank you for bringing Frieda back to us."

For a brief moment, everyone's attention directed at Eleanor. Not at ease with the attention, she lifted her cup high up the air. "Cheers," she said.

"Cheers," resonated the men and women, holding their cups up in the air. Unified.

Eleanor, sitting on a trunk, stared at her drying jacket near the fire. She moved aside for Frieda who snugged up to her.

"Your first?" asked Frieda.

Eleanor looked at Frieda, not knowing for sure what she was asking.

"First time you killed, I meant…"

Eleanor nodded without changing so much as a muscle in her face.

"Well, thank you for that. I'm very happy you did. I wouldn't be here if you didn't," said Frieda.

"I know. No regrets, don't worry, I –"

"I know, give it some time."

They stared into the fire.

"Tell me Eleanor, who's Paul?"

Eleanor held her breath as if she wasn't sure what to tell her. Everything had happened so fast, and she herself was still unsure of what to make of it. It had all been so out of character, all muddled so…

Eleanor refocused on the crackling flames and started talking. She told Frieda about Paul, her husband William, about the blackmail and betrayal.

She talked about how Paul tried to force her to be with him, and how now he told everyone that she was his wife.

Frieda put her arm around Eleanor and pulled her in. "I'm happy you're here with us."

Frieda sat up and opened her torso to turn to lighter conversations. "You made me think I made the worst mistake ever. You were all dressed up," said Frieda, pointing at Eleanor's cloths. "*Strong* Nazi vibe," she blinked, sticking out her tongue in disgust.

"Yeah, I know," grinned Eleanor. "It felt shitty to play along, but it seemed like the smartest thing to do given my situation…"

Frieda bobbed her head, "Most definitely. And now, any plans?" inquired Frieda once again measuring Eleanor up.

"Finding William..." Eleanor responded, "*Just*, finding William. Nothing else."

"Do you know where he is?"

Eleanor nodded, "Auschwitz."

Frieda, tried to hide what she was thinking by echoing "*Auschwitz*." Her posture exposed everything she tried to conceal.

Eleanor, pretending she didn't notice, changed the conversation. "Wasn't it dangerous to have yourself captured and locked in Ravensbrück just to teach the prisoners how to meddle with the weapons?"

"*Just?*" grinned Frieda smoldering with raised brows. "Of course, it was dangerous. But, considering the lives it saved and the lives it took, it was worth it. I'd do it again tomorrow."

Frieda got up as she grazed her hands around Eleanor's shoulders, "Let's talk about it in the morning. Get some sleep, it's going to be a long day."

That night too, Eleanor had to share a bed, but not with three others. She shared a bed with Johan, a real dude, decisive, strong, unconventional with a boyish vibe. When she entered, he spotted her hesitation.

"I'm worried too, you know," he said. "Everybody knows women are only after one thing." He grinned and slapped his buttocks. "Cute touchy right?"

Eleanor wanted to laugh, but she couldn't. She really, *really*, wanted to, but her memories triggered feelings that hit her like a hazel stone falling from a bright blue sky.

The serious look on her face told her story.

Johan, embarrassed, changed his attitude.

"Horrifying experiences with men?" he asked, forward as he was.

"With men? *Yes*. With women, *also* yes, with both actually," she added as she pulled herself together and sat on the other side of the bed.

Johan got up and stuck out his not so tiny pink. "Pinky swear that I won't touch you? I.., I *will* touch you, but not like that. I promise."

Eleanor laughed. His childish gesture and disarming twinkle took away her tension. She crawled into bed and rested her head.

She peaked through an opening in the tent and felt a deep sense of respect. These people weren't living easy lives. Their sacrifice was enormous.

Frieda's brave stories about blown-up bridges and secret missions replayed in her head. Many partisans had died during these missions. Many had been hung, shot or gassed when captured.

She was proud to be among these people.

She crawled closer to Johan. She closed her eyes and listened to the soothing voices of the Partisan's outside of her tent. They put her to sleep as would a love imbued lullaby.

Eleanor woke up early in the morning. It was cold and damp, yet she hopped out of bed and went straight for Frieda. "What are we going to do today," she asked with a certitude that almost made her trip over her own words.

"You are in a decisive mood today," grinned Frieda, as if she had to temper an overly enthusiastic toddler.

"Yes, yes, of course. What can I do?" repeated Eleanor with an inner greed she never knew she had in her. The partisans had inspired her and though she had no clue how to save her husband and all those other people suppressed and enslaved, she knew she had to fight. And, *all* be damned. *Hell*, she was going to. Only this time. This time she had to be prepared. Unprepared statement-actions were not going to cut it. Nothing but a strategy would do.

"Combat training in thirty minutes then," grinned Frieda amazed by this transformation. This was not the sweetheart she had been talking to yesterday. This, for sure, was a woman.

Eleanor was convinced. Even if she wouldn't be helping William right away, she would be soon. He was strong, he would manage to hold on a bit longer. *That,* she was sure of.

For weeks she trained and she loved it. When she was younger, she had been quite athletic, but she kind of slacked off when she had married. Occupied with everyday life, it didn't seem important.

"*Why the hell* did she give it up?" she wondered. "Strange, how you can feel so safe at times, that you never expect to be part of conflict. And then, all of the sudden, you *are*, and it turns out you need skills you never expected."

At one point, she thought that her former efforts had been a complete waste of time. Now she knew, it hadn't.

Her former exertions helped her to regain muscle and condition faster, and, did it. Her whole state-of-being improved. The passion with which she approached combat training, ranging from handling guns to physical fights, was flabbergasting. It was clear to everyone, that besides her physical fitness, her resilience and her long-forgotten sense of self had grown.

The same routines, day after day, didn't bother her. She trained, she volunteered, and brainstormed on how to get William out of Auschwitz. She helped designing strategies to launch attacks, and free as many prisoners as they could.

For weeks she had been asking to join their missions, but time after time, the answer was no, despite that she was sure that she was ready. Ready for whatever mission they would assign.

She and Frieda, had a connection. Every evening they sat together, chatted and brainstormed about potential targets. This evening was no different, wasn't it that Frieda had a different question.

"Ela, do you think you're ready?"

"*Yes*," exclaimed Eleanor without hearing Frida out.

"Really Ela, I don't want to lose you. Hear me out first," protested Frieda.

Eleanor laughed, "I know. I *do* believe I'm ready for whatever it is."

"We'll start with a small mission. We need someone to join Johan to the village. You, with your looks and cloths, would be our safest bet."

"Of course, yes. I said *yes*, right?" laughed Eleanor, happy to finally get some mud on her boots.

"Ease down Ela, or you are no longer our *safest* bet," murmured Frieda annoyed.

The next morning, Eleanor and Johan left for the village. They snugged up like a loving couple, and went undercover as newly-weds. They recently moved, and were in need for arsenic to deal with rats that were overtaking their house.

There weren't any rats in the camp. If there were, they would already have been eaten. The real plan was to put arsenic in bread that was especially baked for Nazi officials. One of the partisan's many cunning plans.

Johan and Eleanor entered the five-and-dime, a shop selling both everything and nothing. It was quite a big store and the atmosphere felt surrealistic. At the cashier's-desk, a gramophone was playing songs that didn't fit the dread of its era. Behind the counter stood a seasoned lady. There was something peculiar about her. I was almost like she came straight out of a comic book. Something about her was rather unsettling. She seemed to be as apathetic as surprised when they entered.

"Guten Tag," said the woman.

"Guten Tag," responded Johan and Eleanor while nodding at her from a distance.

They browsed quietly through the shop.

Passing by the shelves they got a strong sense of being spied on. They pretended they didn't notice, but felt how her prying eyes were staring them down. In every corner and opening between the shelves, she was there.

They tried to ignore it, but when the woman approached, facing them directly, their heart sunk.

"You must have quite some rats," spoke the old lady with a metallic voice, pointing at the cardboard packages of rat poison in their arms.

They smiled and nodded.

The woman smiled too as she squeezed herself through the narrow aisle and pressed her body against Johan's.

Johan looked motionless at Eleanor. He opened his eyes beyond wide and his eyebrows closed the distance to his hairline. "Remember that I told you, women want but one thing?" he smirked.

Eleanor chuckled when she noticed his glowing cheeks.

"She pinched me," he whispered, "in my butt."

Eleanor giggled, "That's why she's spying on us... I'm sorry, I mean... *on you*... Maybe you should cease this opportunity..."

"Ela shut up, *please*," jested Johan poking Eleanor. "It's not like men are always in the mood. We men do have feelings too, you know? We like foreplay too."

At that exact moment, the door opened and two German soldiers marched in with a deck of papers. Johan pulled Eleanor behind the shelves.

"Fraulein, do you recognize this woman?" inquired one of the men rather loud. He handed over a piece of paper. The elderly woman looked at it and shook her head.

"No. I have never seen her," mumbled the woman. "Let me get my husband. He might recognize her."

She called for her husband. It was the onset of slow hobbling feet and the sound of a scraping cane on the floor. Her husband turned out to be an old man. Many years senior to his wife. His face carried a dull know-it-all expression.

He shuffled to the front of the shop and looked at the soldiers. His face lit up and he welcomed them with open arms. Everything in his manners showed he loved to talk to them. He too, had been a soldier once. He battled in the first World War, a fact he was very proud of.

"No, I haven't seen her," said the old man, trying to keep his false teeth in his mouth.

"I'll contact you when I do. What did she do? Is it a rat, a traitor?" he inquired.

As the old man was rattling away telling stories of back in the day, his own wife was standing in front of Eleanor and Johan. She put her finger against her lips to shush them.

"*I know it's you*," she whispered pressing her finger against Eleanor's chest. "*I know it's her,*" she repeated to Johan.

Eleanor tried not to nod.

"I can tell them it's her," she threatened, turning to Johan.

"We'd really hope you wouldn't," he whispered.

The tone of her voice changed, "How bad don't you want me to tell it?"

Eleanor and Johan looked at each other. They didn't know what to make of this strange threat. What was she saying?

The woman stepped forward and pressed her body against Johan's. She put both her hands on his chest, and rubbed his pectorals. She barely looked at him. She just unbuttoned his coat and put her hands on his bare skin.

He looked her. He wasn't used to not being in control. He could snap her neck in a blink of a second, yet he was at her will.

Eleanor interfered by stepping between them, but the woman, not impressed at all, focused on Johan's posture. She touched him like she hadn't touched a man in years.

"Touch me," she whispered, soft enough to stay below the gramophone's pitch. "Touch me. Kiss me. *Here*, grab my buttocks," she said turning her rear towards him.

Eleanor stepped forward and placed her hand on the woman's shoulder. "Please, don't do this," she insisted.

She couldn't let this happen to Johan. She had been in his shoes. She *had* to make it stop. She didn't want to be arrested, but nobody would have to go through this on *her* behalf.

She raised her hand to speak up, but Johan shushed her.

"Ela, don't do it. It's ok. Let her," he whispered, gesturing her to calm down. He was fully aware of the consequences of her arrest. "Let me do this for you. Just go to the next aisle. I will be with you in a moment."

Tormented, and disappointed in herself, she walked to the next aisle. She was still in plain view of what was happening. She saw how the woman rubbed Johan all over his body. How eager she took off his coat and how she went straight for his zipper. She pulled his face towards hers, and French-kissed him. She pushed her tongue into his mouth and started sucking.

Uncomfortable with the duckface gulping up his mouth, Johan clamped his lips together.

He had to man himself up to let her touch him. Johan looked up and met Eleanor's eyes. He smiled at her, searching for her warmth, her heart, for contact.

She knew like no other what he was going through. She understood he needed something to hold on to. She needed it too, during the cold nights she spent in Ravensbrück's barracks. William had helped *her* through. Now Johan was looking for something to cling to. This was what she could give him, it was what she wanted to give him.

She looked at him, and made sure her eyes twinkled. She removed the pin from her bonnet so her hair dropped loosely on her back. She lifted her shoulders, bold and sexy, and touched her lips with her finger, capturing his eyes with hers. She looked coy and naughty, and played her femininity by tilting her head while smiling. She moved her hips in circles, caressing her body with her hands.

She touched her hips, her breasts, her neck and curled her hair while holding on to his gaze.

Johan smiled at her and sent her a kiss. "Thank you, Ela," he whispered.

The elderly woman, only 30 feet away from her husband, held on to him. She touched him everywhere before putting her hand in his trousers. She would have never pulled it off, if it wasn't for the gramophone player, playing *I don't want to set the world on fire*...

The woman turned around and bent over. She looked back over her shoulder, inviting Johan to proceed.

"I want to feel you," she whispered, impatient for Johan's next steps. Johan looked at her. He saw a woman with pain and grayed passion in her eyes. Disappointed in life, in need of affection.

He glanced back at Eleanor who was still trying to make things better, as he realized he didn't want to this to either of the women.

He didn't want Ela to go through this kind of harassment, even if it was non-physical. And the shattered woman in front of him... she...

Johan smiled at Eleanor and whispered that he would be all right. He broke eye contact with her and focused on the woman, awaiting his loving affection. He caressed her back and rubbed her shoulders, and noticed how her every movement was a direct response to his touch.

He lifted her dress and squeezed her buttocks. She let out a sigh she was unable to suppress. She tried to inhibit her moans by squeezing her legs with her nails, leaving her own skin with red imprints.

Johan bent over behind her and kissed her neck while pulling her torso upright.

She cast him a glance over her shoulder and showed how much she was craving him. Her unexpected meek look, touched his heart. He smiled at her before opening his zipper. He took out his cock and rubbed it between her soft and warm lips.

His cock grew upon touching her wet pussy. He bent over to rub her pussy lips with circling movements. His strong fingers delved around her clit displaying his experience. With ease, she arched her back. She bent like a cat stretching in front of its owner, lenient as a teenager, thanking him for his touch.

Her movements aroused him in a way he could never have imagined. Her hips grinded his pelvis. Her waist, begging for his touch, invited him to hold her tighter, and the sweet salty smell of her wet cunt seduced his cock like spring blossom lures in bumblebees.

Though her body screamed for more attention, he no longer wanted to wait. Her body cringed as he pressed his dick inside of her, and he bit his lips as his dick filled her tight neglected cunt. He loved her wetness and heat, her uninhibited begging for his sex and her full surrender upon receiving what she pleaded for.

The old man was still flooding the soldiers with endless war stories of his time. Though he never seemed to end his conversation, it was a dangerous game.

It was not time that spurred Johan though. It was lust that provoked him to poke her with deep thrusting impacts.

Her ass slammed against his pelvis and he loved its softness and how it bounced back after impact. This, was a real woman. A woman with boobies that he could hold, squeeze and fondle. A woman with soft skin, yet not so soft that would make a man afraid to bruise it. A woman unashamed of her lustfulness.

His hands pressed and pulled her in, while his cock grinded itself into her ribbed pussy flesh. Her tight pussy-muscles clamped on to him to prevented his cock from leaving.

He fucked her and stroked her slit until she was shaking from the overpowering strength of orgasm. Her trembling body was his signal. He let go and released his warm cum in her lustful snatch. With his cock still inside of her he embraced her, and hugged her out of loving passion.

He caressed her, and helped her straighten her cloths. The woman was silent. She just looked at him with widened pupils, as if the soft touch of heaven had finally found a way to earth.

"I'm sorry, but we need to go," he whispered. He locked his eyes onto hers, anticipating her disappointment.

For a second, she looked at him hopeful, as if 'we' included her in his story.

She nodded as she realized it wasn't him and her, but that they had to go.

With a pained smile, she led them to an exit in the back. She grabbed his hand and held it between hers like she was afraid this had been the last time she'd ever touch someone.

"Take what you need," she said with a warmth in her voice and an expression in her eyes that was nothing like when they entered the store.

Johan kissed her on the forehead. "Take care?" he asked.

He glanced at her over his shoulders as they walked out the door.

She smiled and blew him a kiss.

They got into to car and drove back to camp.

"Thank you," said Eleanor, touching Johan's hand without actually groping it.

"Thank you too," replied Johan. "I know what you tried to do there. It was really sweet."

"I'm so sorry Johan, I—"

"Don't be, it wasn't your fault. Besides, it wasn't that bad."

"Johan be serious," grinned Eleanor.

Johan pulled up his shoulders, "She had some issues, like most wo—"

"*Some issues?*" frowned Eleanor.

"Just leave it at that, Ela, can you?"

Eleanor was silent. Nothing more needed to be said. Both of them knew.

Upon arrival, the camp was in chaos. People were packing, breaking down tents and running around in blind panic.

Johan and Eleanor tried to stop people to ask what was going on, but everyone was too busy.

Finally, they managed to find Frieda.

"Frieda, what is –"

"Ela, they are looking for you. We need to clear the camp and set base elsewhere. Those fucking Nazis are about to sweep the whole god damn forest."

"But what about our plans?" inquired Eleanor.

"Postpone them. Cancel them. Whatever, but for now, *hurry*."

"I can turn myself in," said Eleanor.

"*We're not even going to consider that!*" replied Johan. "Just *pack* Eleanor."

"Frieda, *you* are rational. You *know* we *should consider it.* The only reason that they are sweeping the forest is that Paul is looking for me. If it wasn't for him, nobody would care. I can go back to Ravensbrück. I'll claim you kidnapped me. You fucked up and I managed to escape…"

"And then what? Even *if* they would believe you… Ela, come on. What about the dead soldier? What about Paul?" interfered Johan agitated.

"I can handle Paul. Besides, think of all the things I can do on the inside. Think of all the advantages. I can sabotage them, we won't lose time rebuilding the camp, *and* you can execute our plans as scheduled…"

Eleanor knew she had their full attention, even though they didn't like it.

"Either of you would sacrifice your live. So, why not me?"

"Because I don't want you to," said Johan. "You *do* know what will happen if we continue with our plan when you're in there? Retribution. *Unequal retribution.* For every casualty on their side, they'll kill hundreds of ours. *I don't want you in there.*"

"Johan, for one, I won't be considered one of *them*, and second, is my life worth more than theirs? They are killing us anyway. I know what you did for me and I'm beyond grateful, but we *can* turn this into our advantage."

Both Frieda and Johan knew Eleanor was right. They hated it, but logic and reason dictated that Eleanor would go back to the Nazi compound. That same night.

The three of them entered a truck and drove in the direction of Ravensbrück. Eleanor knew she had to be convincing. She had to look like an escaped prisoner of war, and like the others, she knew what that meant.

Still miles away from Ravensbrück they got out of the car.

"Don't worry. Don't think about it. Just do it," comforted Eleanor, looking at their tormented faces.

Frieda held her close. "*Sorry*," she whispered. Frieda ripped up Eleanor's cloths, pushed her away and stumped her in her stomach. Johan, for the first time without a beaming smile, closed his eyes and elbowed Eleanor in her face. Eleanor's lips and cheeks twitched as drops of blood ran down her nose. All of them were tormented. They had grown so close in so little time, and now they had to leave their third musketeer at the lion's den. At her own. At the will of a beast.

Eleanor reassured them and flipped her inner-switch. She turned around and ran. She ran and ran without looking back.

She stumbled for miles over rocks and barely touched trails, hidden under leaves and branches. Thorns scratched her skin, which – in her eyes – only helped her look her part.

She came closer to the inhabited world, and the closer she came, the emptier she felt. She became ultra-aware of her surroundings. The whistling leaves. The cold wind on her skin. Her freezing hands. None of it bothered her. She knew what she was about to do, and why. She was strong and on a mission.

She drew closer and could see the lights of the compound flickering between the trees. How on earth was she going to deal with Paul?

She hated everything about him and now she was going to pretend to be his wife. To want him, to be with him, to...

She stopped running.

In front of her, separated by a mere hundred yards, the iron gate of Ravensbrück. Her heart hammered in her chest. Alone in the cold darkness, everything became real.

She thought about her William and what *he* was going through, and she thought about herself, and what *she* would be going through. The future was still unwritten, but of one thing she was sure. She was *done* being a victim. She was a soldier now. It didn't matter what Paul or anyone else was going to do to her. She *would* be able to handle it.

Without further delay, she walked towards the gate, and knocked on the iron barred door.

She was ready for this.

She could *endure it*. She would *endure it*.

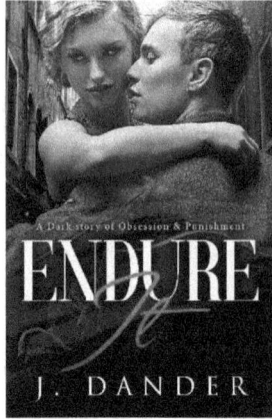

Endure It – a dark story of obsession and punishment

Would you walk the road to freedom if it was paved with sacrifices?
Eleanor had it all figured out. She would pose as Officer Jordan's wife and manipulate him into freeing her husband. She never expected the *other* monster to interfere. A monster, that was not willing to give her up without a fight...

*The Endure Series are **Black label** books. They contain steamy sex scenes, violence, BDSM, and other thematic content. Classified as a romantic thriller / historical drama set in WOII. **Reader discretion is advised**.*

You can write about things you don't believe in.
You can crave for things you never want to live.
Fight the reality.
Don't cage my fantasy...

Hello!

Thank you for reading *Endure Him*. I hope you enjoyed it so far.

I didn't expect it to come out this dark, so I'd love to know what you think.
Was it too much? Were there parts you liked or hated?
I would really appreciate it if you'd share your thoughts. :)

As you may know, it's impossible to advertise dark books like these, so it's hard to get this book to readers. What would help enormously is if you could write a review. It is alright to think this book is good, bad or ugly. I'm already grateful that you took the time to give me your feedback.

Love and kisses,

Jonna

E-mail: jonna@jdander.com
Instagram: https://www.instagram.com/j.dander/
Website: www.tedantpublishing.com
Amazon Author page: https://www.amazon.com/-/e/B07MH3ETYB

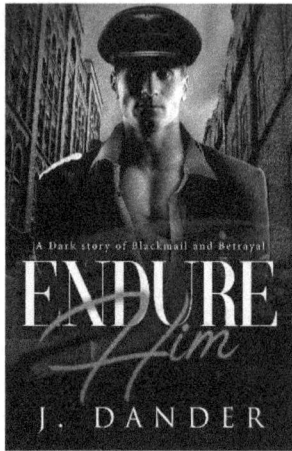

Endure Him – A Dark Story of Blackmail and Betrayal

<u>Endure Him – A Dark Story of Blackmail and Betrayal</u>

How far would you go for the man you love?

Eleanor's husband is hiding from the Nazis. When his secret hiding place is detected by her former boyfriend, Nazi Officer Jordan, her husband's life is at stake. *She* is the only one that is able to stop her ex from betraying him.

Officer Jordan promises to keep her secret, but his services don't come cheap. He wants something in return. *He wants her. All of her.* Her body, her mind, her soul. What started with *just a kiss* plunged down the rabbit hole. How far will he go to have her to himself? How far will *she* go to protect the man she loves?

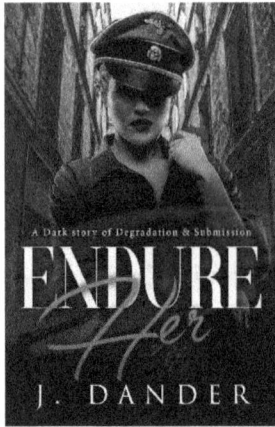

Endure Her – A Dark Story of Degradation and Submission

How do you bear the unbearable?

After defying her abuser, Eleanor never expected her life to take a turn for the worst. She is sent to camp Ravensbrück, where one of the sadistic female guards takes a special interest in her.

All Eleanor wanted is to be reunited with her beloved husband. All she got, was bone-chilling abuse that forced her to submit to a woman that knew no mercy. A woman that craved to dominate her. Devour her. *All* of her.

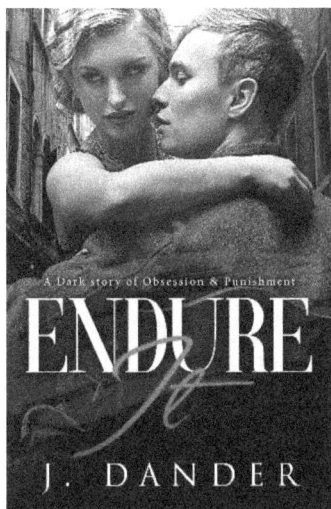

Endure It – a dark story of obsession and punishment

Would you walk the road to freedom if it was paved with sacrifices?

Eleanor had it all figured out. She would pose as Officer Jordan's wife and manipulate him into freeing her husband. She never expected the *other* monster to interfere. A monster, that was not willing to give her up without a fight...

The Endure Series are Black label books. They contain steamy sex scenes, violence, BDSM, and other thematic content. Classified as a romantic thriller / drama set in WOII. Reader discretion is advised.

Other reads by Jonna

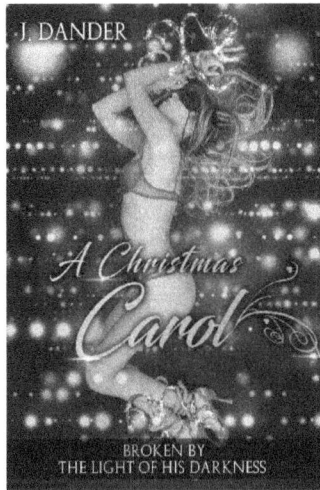

A Christmas Carol – Broken by the light of his darkness

Jesse, a top graduated lawyer, is living the good life. When the handsome stranger Mr. Duncan enters her life, she immediately knows he's the one. He is strong, dominant, and sexy, and despite his dark side, he is everything she ever wished for, or so she thinks...

A Christmas Carol – Broken by the light of his darkness, is a standalone - dark Christmas tale, set in the rich circles of New

York. It contains everything you may expect of dark BDSM erotica in a Christmas setting. It's mysterious, humorous, and troubling, and above all: kinky and sexy alpha-males.

CPSIA information can be obtained
at www.ICGtesting.com
Printed in the USA
LVHW091417311220
675533LV00032B/347